ENDANGERED!

WHALES

Johannah Haney

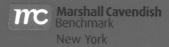

Marshall Cavendish
Benchmark

New York

Marshall Cavendish Benchmark
99 White Plains Road
Tarrytown, New York 10591
www.marshallcavendish.us

Editor: Karen Ang
Publisher: Michelle Bisson
Art Director: Anahid Hamparian
Series Design by: Elynn Cohen
Cover Design by Kay Petronio

Library of Congress Cataloging-in-Publication Data

Haney, Johannah.
Whales / by Johannah Haney.
p. cm. -- (Endangered!)
Includes bibliographical references and index.
Summary: "Describes the characteristics, behavior, and plight of
endangered whale species, and what people can do to help"--Provided by
publisher.
ISBN 978-0-7614-2990-6
1. Whales--Juvenile literature. 2. Endangered species--Juvenile literature. I. Title.
QL737.C4H256 2009
599.5--dc22   2008023374

Front cover: A humpback whale
Back cover: A humpback whale mother and calf (top); A bowhead whale (bottom)

Photo research by Pamela Mitsakos
Front cover: Brandon Cole / Alamy

The photographs in this book are used by permission and through the courtesy of:
Peter Arnold: BIOS / Brandon Cole, 1; Douglas Seifert - UNEP, 4; Steven Kazlowski, 9; Michael Nolan, 11; Stephen Wong,
12; Marilyn Kazmers, 16; I Everson/WWI, 18; Jonathan Bird, 26; P. Wegner, 27; Kelvin Aitken, 31; Sea Life Surveys, 32;
Biosphoto, 38. Photo Researchers: Michael Patrick O'Neill, 7, back cover (top); Bud Lehnhausen, 8; Joyce Photographics,
10; Francois Gohier, 14, 22, 44; Stephen Krasemann, 15. Animals Animals - Earth Scenes: James Watt, 20. Minden
Pictures: Martha Holmes, 24, back cover (bottom). SuperStock: Image Asset Management, Ltd., 28. AP Images: Brad
Nettles/Associated Press, 35, 42. Peter Lennihan/Associated Press, 36; Katsumi Kasahara/Associated Press, 40; Linda
Richter/Associated Press, 41; Michael Dinneen/Associated Press, 43.

Printed in China
1 2 3 4 5 6

Contents

1

The Lives of Whales

A huge gray-colored whale leaps out of the water and makes a graceful arc through the air. With a *SPLASH* it lands in the ocean followed by an enormous spray of water. Nearby, another whale peeks its head out of the water and spins in a full circle to check out its surroundings. Another whale comes to the surface and water gushes high into the air from its **blowhole.** These are all common activities of some of the Earth's largest animals— the whales.

A sperm whale dives down to join the rest of its group after leaping out of the water and splashing back in.

Whales are fascinating creatures, with interesting physical features, unique survival abilities, and intriguing habits. Scientists still have a lot to learn about whales, but sadly, many types of whales have become **endangered**. Some types have already become **extinct**, or have disappeared forever.

WHALE BODIES

When talking about whales, many scientists often use the word **cetaceans.** There are about eighty different **species,** or types, of cetaceans, including dolphins and porpoises. (Dolphins and porpoises are not whales, but they are related to them.) Because whales live in water, sometimes people think they are a type of fish, but they are not. Whales are mammals, like humans, which means they are warm-blooded (they control their body temperature internally), have at least a little hair, give birth to live babies instead of laying eggs, and feed their young with milk from a mother.

By definition, all mammals have hair, but it is obvious that whales are not covered in fur! Most baby whales have a few whiskers on their head. Most lose these hairs, but humpback whales keep these hairs, which might help them be more aware of their surroundings, much like a cat uses its whiskers.

Whales need to breathe air, just like other mammals that live on land. But unlike other types of mammals, whales can hold their breath underwater for an amazingly long time. A male sperm whale can hold its breath for more than two hours, while other types of whales can hold their breath for several minutes. When a whale dives under the water, its body saves up air the air it needs to breathe. Its heart rate slows down, so that its body uses less air. A whale breathes by coming to the surface of the water and exhaling, or blowing out air, through its blowhole. A blowhole for a whale is like the nostrils at the end of your nose. The whale's blowhole is located on the top of its head. When a whale exhales through its blowhole, a spray of water vapor and mucus (a sticky body fluid) shoots up into the air. This is called a blow or spout. The blow of some species of whales can be seen from miles away.

Many scientists and whale watchers locate whales by keeping an eye out for spouts or blows.

Thick layers of blubber beneath their skin keep these orcas, or killer whales, warm in the freezing waters of the Arctic.

Whales have a thick layer of fat under their skin called **blubber.** Blubber is very important to whales because it keeps them warm in cold waters. It is also where whales store extra fat to use as energy during long periods when they are traveling to new waters, or **migrating.** Blubber also helps whales to float. Unfortunately, their blubber was one of the reasons why so many whales have been killed. In the past, hunters used whale blubber for fuel and for things like soap.

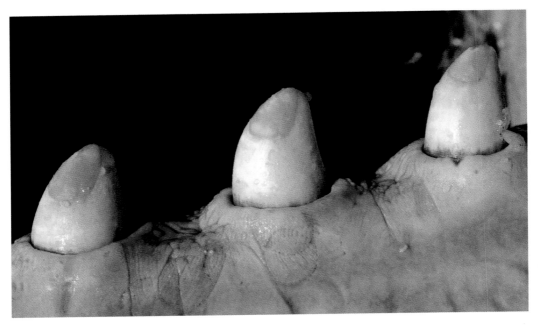

They may not look very sharp, but these teeth can be deadly when their size and shape are combined with the biting strength of a toothed whale's jaw.

FOOD

Different types of whales eat different kinds of food. Toothed whales eat squid, fish, and other kinds of marine mammals. These types of whales have cone-shaped teeth that are strong and sharp. Whales without teeth have a curtain of hard, hornlike material coming down from their upper jaw. This is called **baleen.** Whales that have baleen instead of teeth are called baleen whales. Baleen whales

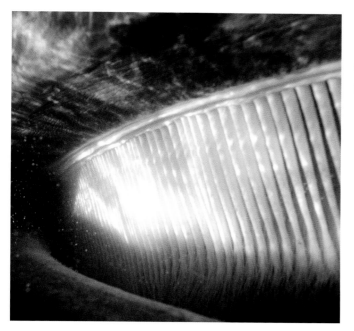

Bristles on baleen plates help to catch the whale's food.

are filter feeders, which means they eat very small marine life. As water—and the little creatures swimming in it—passes into the whale's mouth, the baleen filters out the food from the water.

MIGRATION

Many cetaceans, especially baleen whales, migrate each year. They move to colder waters during summer to feed and store fat for the winter. Then, in the colder months of the year, they move to warmer waters to breed and give birth. Some whales migrate as far as 5,000 miles (8,047 kilometers) each way!

Along the United States, whales migrate along both the east and west coast. For example, during late summer, gray whales on the west coast, stay near the Alaskan coast of the Bering Sea. But in the winter, they

As they migrate from the north, a group of whales swims through the warmer waters off the coast of the Hawaiian Islands.

move to the warmer waters around Baja, California, to breed. On the east coast during the summer, north Atlantic right whales feed off the coasts of Maine, Massachusetts, and Nova Scotia in Canada. In winter, these right whales travel to the coasts of Georgia and Florida to breed and give birth to baby whales, which are called **calves.**

SOCIAL LIFE AND COMMUNICATION

Whales are very social animals. This means that they interact with each other a lot. Whales often travel in groups called **pods.** Pods usually include between five and thirty whales. However, some pods can be quite large and may include hundreds of whales. Whales communicate with each other using whistles, clicks, chirps, and screams. They can tell each other where food is located, warn members of their pod about dangers ahead, and ask for help if they are sick or injured. These behaviors help the whales stay safe as they travel in groups. However, it has also made them easier targets for whalers, or people

A gray whale spyhops to check out its surroundings.

who hunt whales. When whales travel in pods, it is easier for whalers to hunt a whole group of whales at once.

Some types of whales stand upright in the water to look for other whales, boats or animals on the surface of the water. By turning around, they can see what is all around them. This is called spyhopping. Another whale activity is called breaching. Breaching occurs when a whale jumps out of the water and lands with an enormous splash. No one knows for sure why whales breach, but some people who study whales think they might be trying to attract a mate, look for other whales, or confuse their **prey.** Whales also engage in lobtailing. Lobtailing is when a whale sticks its tail out of the water and slaps it onto the surface of the water, creating a spray. Like breaching, scientists do not know exactly why whales do this. They think it might be one way for whales to warn other whales about danger.

Lobtailing may be one of many ways that whales communicate with each other.

2

Whales of the World

Whales live in all of the world's oceans. Different types prefer certain regions of the world. They also have different habits and ways of interacting with each other and with other animals. Many types of whales are endangered or **threatened.**

BALEEN WHALES

Baleen whales that are endangered or threatened include humpback, bowhead, blue, gray, and fin whales. These whales have two blowholes on top of their heads. If

A gray whale calf pops out of the water before diving back down to join its mother and the rest of the pod.

Different types of krill can range in size—from less than half an inch to about 5 inches.

you were on a beach and you saw two great plumes of water spray into the air at the same time, they most likely came from a baleen whale. Toothed whales only have one blowhole.

Baleen whales eat mostly **krill,** which are small, shrimplike creatures that live in polar waters. To eat their food, baleen whales use a few different methods. Some whales, such as the gray whale, go to the ocean floor and suck in mouthfuls of dirt and water. They use their baleen to filter out small animals like crabs. Other whales swim along the surface of the water with their mouths open. The bristly parts of the baleen catch krill and other small creatures, which are then swallowed. Other baleen whales take in giant mouthfuls of water. They then use their tongues to push the water out while the food gets trapped in the baleen. Though there are many of them in the water, krill are very small. Because whales are so large, they need to spend most of their day eating so that they have enough energy to survive.

During the colder months of the year, baleen whales migrate to warmer waters. There, they breed and give birth. When a calf is born, its mother helps it to the surface to breathe in air. Even months after it is born, a calf may swim right above its mother, so that she can help the baby go up to get air. Calves can also rest on their mothers' backs and fins when they need help swimming. For food, calves start out drinking their mother's nutritious milk. After a while, they learn to filter feed using their baleen. A whale calf nurses for up to a year before eating solid food.

Right Whales

When whale hunting (whaling) was very common, this type of whale got its name because it was the "right" type of whale to hunt. Because it is a slow swimmer, travels close to shore, floats when it is dead, and provides a lot of oil, whalers targeted the north Atlantic right whale. That is a major reason why north Atlantic right whales are endangered today. Scientists estimate that about 350 north Atlantic right whales remain today. The southern right whale, which lives in the southern hemisphere, is in less danger. There are about 1,500 southern right whales remaining today.

If the laws protecting right whales are not enforced, and conservation efforts do not continue, northern Atlantic right whales will disappear from the oceans.

Female right whales only breed once every three to five years. As a result, right whale populations take time to grow. Although hunting right whales is against the law in most places, the whales still face a lot of dangers. Many whales get trapped in fishing nets meant for other fish. When the whales get tangled, they drown or injure themselves while struggling. Right whales are also affected by pollution and collisions with ships.

Blue Whales

The blue whale is a baleen whale, and it is the largest animal that lives on Earth today. A blue whale can grow to be 100 feet (30 m) long and can weigh as much as 150 tons (136 tonnes). In the summer, when the blue whale is feeding to save energy for the winter migration, it can eat as many as 40 million krill each day.

Blue whales have also been affected by the whaling industry. In 1931, when whaling was more common, nearly 30,000 blue whales were killed in a single season. Most of the blue whales that remain today are a subspecies—a specific type of species—called pygmy blue whales. As their name suggests, these whales are smaller than

Several species of whales, including the blue whale, are called rorquals because they have a series of folds in the skin extending from the mouth to the belly. These folds expand to allow more water and food into the whale's mouth.

regular blue whales. Scientists believe that around 500 true, huge blue whales living around Antarctica are the last of their kind.

Humpback Whales

Humpback whales enchant people with their playful breaching, their fascinating mating calls, and frequent tail lobbing. Researchers have had great success studying the humpback whale in its wild habitat. This is because each humpback has a unique pattern on its fin and flippers to help identify it. This is a lot like human fingerprints—no two people have the same fingerprints. Because of this, scientists are able to track individual humpbacks to learn about their migration, mating, and other behaviors.

In the early days of whaling, many humpbacks were killed, but the species has slowly started to recover. The humpback whale is currently vulnerable to endangerment. That means that it is not currently classified as endangered, but conservationists are watching them to make sure they remain safe from extinction.

Bowhead Whales

The bowhead whale is found in the icy waters in the Arctic. They are able to use the tops of their heads to break through ice that can be up to 2 feet (61 cm) deep in order to breathe. To stay warm in icy cold water, bowhead whales have a layer of blubber that can be 2 feet (61 cm) thick.

The baleen of these whales is the longest of all whales—about 14 feet (4.3 m) long. This made the bowhead whale a popular choice for whalers who hunted for

The bowhead gets its name from the shape of its huge mouth. The whale's lower jaw is curved in such a way that it looks like the shape of a bow that is used to shoot arrows.

baleen. Hunting the bowhead whale is illegal, but native people like the Inuit who live along the Arctic coast are allowed to kill a certain number of bowhead whales each year for food and oil. There are about 8,000 bowhead whales alive today.

TOOTHED WHALES

Besides using their eyes, this type of whale also uses special senses to help them navigate through the water.

Toothed whales use **echolocation** to help them find food and know what is up ahead. Here is how it works. A whale lets out stream of sounds from its melon, which is a small bump on its forehead. The sounds hit anything around the whale and send back signals that are like an echo. The whale can sense the echo and pinpoint the size and location of things in its surroundings. Echolocation is very precise. Whales can detect something that is less than a half inch (1.27 centimeters) in size from a distance of 50 feet (15 meters). Some toothed cetaceans with poor eyesight, such as river dolphins, use echolocation almost exclusively to hunt and avoid obstacles. Other animals, such as bats, use echolocation in the air.

Because baleen whales were hunted more than toothed whales, not as many toothed whale species are endangered. The sperm whale is a toothed species that was once the prime target for whalers in the eighteenth and nineteenth centuries. They can grow to be 50 to 60 feet (15.2 to 18.3 m). These big-headed whales were hunted for blubber and for the spermaceti material in its head. This substance was used for fuel, makeup

A snorkeler swims next to a sperm whale. In most cases, whales will ignore humans that are swimming nearby.

ingredients, and other oil products. Its blubber was used for fuel, and material called ambergris was taken from the whale's digestive tract. Ambergris was and is a popular ingredient in perfumes. Today the sperm whale is listed as endangered, though its worldwide numbers are higher than other those of other whales.

Orcas, or killer whales, are another type of toothed whale that is in danger. Killer whales get their name from the fact that they are very good hunters. These whales,

In sea parks, killer whales breach and do tricks to entertain and educate humans. In the wild, these activities may be for communication or to hunt prey.

which can grow to be 30 feet (9.1 m), are able to hunt down seals and other whales. Some orcas even work together to hunt larger whales. Orcas in general are not listed as endangered, but certain pods in parts of the world, such as those in Puget Sound off the coast of Washington state, are protected by laws like the Endangered Species Act. These whales are small in number not because of over-hunting, but because of habitat destruction and loss of prey. The waters they live in have been polluted and there are fewer fish for them to eat. Local laws and other efforts have been made to help protect this whale.

3

In Danger

WHALING

One of the biggest reasons why so many whales are endangered today is whaling, or hunting whales for food and material. Many historians believe that people have been hunting whales for more than 7,000 years. Whales have been used for their meat, blubber, baleen plates, and skin.

Over time, the techniques for hunting whales have improved. Around the twelfth century, Japanese whalers began using a harpoon, which is a spear-like weapon attached to a rope. Whalers would throw the harpoon

An illustration from the 1800s shows a crew of whalers hunting down a sperm whale.

into the side of a whale, then pull on the rope to drag the dead body into the boat. Through the years, many changes were made to the harpoon to make it more effective at killing and collecting whales. For example, the toggling harpoon has an extra point that twists in the whale's body. This makes it almost impossible for the harpoon to be pulled out of the whale while whalers are trying to drag the animal into their boat.

In 1865, a whaler from Norway invented the exploding harpoon. This harpoon had a spear that broke into pieces once it was inside the whale. This made sure that the whale was seriously injured or dead so that collecting the body was easier. Improving boats also made it easier for whalers to go farther out to sea to hunt.

Why were people so interested in hunting whales? Many different things could be made from the body of a whale. Of course, people wanted the meat for food. But other parts of the whale were useful, too. Baleen was used to make corsets—an undergarment designed to shape women's waists—umbrellas, lampshades, and other decorative items. The oil taken from whale's blubber was used to light lamps for heat and light, to make products such as lipstick, shoe polish, soap, ink, and even oil for food ingredients such as margarine.

In the last century, new substances and technologies have replaced the use of many whale parts. For example, different kinds of non-whale oils have replaced whale oil in many cosmetic and food prod-ucts. New ways of using steel

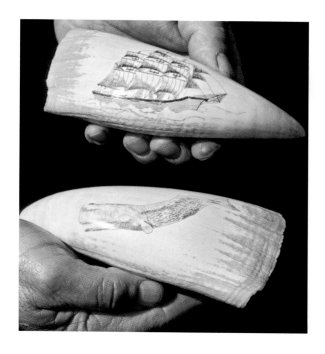

Whaling ships, whales, and other illustrations were often carved into whale teeth or bones and then sold as decorative pieces.

and other strong materials have replaced using baleen. And electricity has replaced lamp oil. But the damage to many whale populations had already been done.

POLLUTION

Pollution of the oceans has had a huge impact on whales and other water creatures. Chemicals such as pesticides (used to kill animals that affect crops or humans), motor

Garbage and other waste products can injure or kill marine life. This whale has a plastic strap stuck in its skin. The plastic is blocking the whale's blowhole, making it hard to breathe.

oil, and even household cleaners end up in the ocean. Small marine animals, such as krill and fish, eat these pollutants. Sometimes these small marine animals die from pollution, which means less food for whales to eat to stay alive. Other times, these marine animals live, but are contaminated, or poisoned, by pollution. When whales eat this prey, they can get sick and even die. Some scientists say that whales are developing diseases like cancer far more than ever, and pollution is likely to blame.

Whales are exposed to so much pollution that it may be dangerous for people who still eat whale meat. Whale meat is a favorite food in Japan. Scientists performed studies on whale meat sold in Japan and found the levels of mercury—a metal that can be poisonous to humans—

were up to 5,000 times higher than is safe. Whales get this mercury into their bodies when they eat fish that are contaminated with mercury from pollution.

Large oil tankers that carry huge amounts of oil are also to blame for pollution in the water. These ships leak oil or crash into reefs, coasts, or ice, dirtying the oceans and seas. The oil kills and sickens many species, which affects animals all the way up the food chain. Cleaning up the spilled oil is very hard, and sometimes it takes years before the water is healthy enough for animals to survive.

Another major source of pollution that affects whales is noise pollution. Noise from large boat engines and sonar from military ships and submarines can harm whales. Sonar is a method of sending out sound signals and measuring the time it takes to echo back. This helps people locate things underwater. It works just the same way that a toothed whale's echolocation works. Some of the sounds that damage whales are at a very low frequency, which means we may not be able to hear the noise, but the whales can. Whales rely on sound to help them find food, communicate with each other, and navigate. When loud sounds disrupt a whale's ability to communicate or navigate, they sometimes try to get away from the noise.

As a result, the migration patterns of some types of whales have been changing in areas with a lot of noise pollution. Many whales have also gotten lost and end up beaching themselves. When a whale is beached, it swims too close to the shore and gets stuck on land. The whale cannot get the food it needs, and its skin quickly dries out. Many beached whales die before humans can help them get back out to sea. Some scientists have also found signs that sonar might actually damage the organs (body parts) inside the whale. Laws are in place that control how and where sonar is used.

FISHING

The biggest threat most cetaceans face in most of the world today is getting trapped in fishing nets. Fisheries set up nets and other traps to catch tuna and other fish, but sometimes cetaceans get caught in these traps by mistake. Any animal that is caught in a fishing trap not meant for it is called **bycatch.** When a cetacean is caught

A north Altantic right whale is tangled up in a fiishing net off the coast of North Carolina. Animal rescuers attempted to free the whale, but it could not get loose, and eventually drowned.

in fishing nets as bycatch, it often cannot break free to go to the surface to breathe. The animal drowns. Larger whales can often break free of the nets, but the process can injure the whale and it might die from those injuries. Sometimes when a whale does untangle itself from a net, there is rope or fishing line trapped in its baleen and it has trouble eating. It is hard to know exactly how many whales die like this since not all fisheries report bycatch, and some whales die after they break free of fishing nets. However, some **conservationists** estimate that as many as 308,000 whales die worldwide as a result of bycatch each year. That is about one whale every two minutes.

4

Saving the Whales

People from around the world first began working together to protect whales in 1931. Several countries made efforts to preserve the whale populations that still existed. In 1937, nine countries, including the United States, signed the International Agreement for the Regulation of Whaling. This agreement set limits on whaling. In 1946, the most important advancement in whale conservation occurred when forty-two nations signed the International Convention for the Regulation of Whaling. This agreement also set limits on whaling, and has been updated throughout time to stay up-to-date with changes

Whale-watching tours help raise awareness for the problems the whales face. However, some experts think that too many whale-watching boats can interfere with and harm the wild whales.

in the world. For example, one change was to include people trying to hunt whales in helicopters as "whale-catchers" so they would also have to follow the rules.

The International Convention for the Regulation of Whaling also set up a group to monitor whale populations throughout the world. This group is called the International Whaling Commission (IWC). The IWC reviews and makes changes to the International Convention for the Regulation

Some native peoples are permitted to hunt non-endangered whales since it is a big part of their culture and method of survival. Native hunters usually only catch as many whales as they can use. They do not kill as many whales as commercial whaling companies.

of Whaling when changes are needed. In 1986, the IWC banned commercial whaling altogether. (Commercial whaling involves having many ships hunt and kill large numbers of whales. The whale parts are then sold for money.) The IWC also sets up sanctuaries for whales. In an area set aside as a whale sanctuary, no one can use fishing nets that whales might get trapped in.

CONSERVATION TODAY

Today, a ban on commercial whaling is still in place. However, some countries want to end this ban. Japan, Norway, and Iceland all want to continue whaling because they feel that it is important to their economy.

Japan still catches many whales each year for scientific research, which is allowed under IWC rules. But many conservation groups say that in some cases, "scientific research" is being used as an excuse for some people in Japan to kill whales for food and profit. Between 1,000 and 1,500 whales are killed in Japan's research programs each year. When these whales are killed, the meat is sold in Japanese markets and restaurants for people to eat.

Canned whale meat is sold in an Asian market.

The IWC says that any whales killed for scientific research should be used for food and other practical things, so that no part of the whale is wasted. The Japanese government says hunting and eating whale is part of their cultural heritage, and other countries do not have the right to judge them. None of the types of whales Japan catches are endangered species, but if too many are caught the populations could become dangerously low.

Within the United States, there are many groups that are working to conserve whales today. They try to educate people about endangered whales and help to pass laws to protect them. Many of these organizations focus on keeping whales safe from fishing nets.

The World Wildlife Fund (WWF) is one such organization. In 2002, the WWF formed the International Cetacean Bycatch Task Force. This group works with

A collision with large ships and fast boats can lead to a tragic end for many whales. Special boating rules and protected whale sanctuaries should help prevent occurrences such as these.

fisheries to help them develop fishing nets that are safe for cetaceans. Their efforts have been successful in the past. For example, in 2003, the WWF and other conservation groups worked successfully with the Canadian government to make new traffic patterns for boats that before were disrupting north Atlantic right whales' feeding grounds.

Save the Whales is another conservation group in the United States. The goal of this organization is to educate people about whales and the condition of the oceans they live in. Save the Whales was started in 1977 by a fourteen-year-old girl named Maris Sidenstecker. As an adult, she still runs the organization today. The organization helps educate people about the effects of noise pollution, chemical pollution in storm water drains that ends up in the ocean, the cruelty of keeping whales in captivity, and many other issues that whales face.

HOW YOU CAN HELP

Everyone can help save the whales. Buying canned tuna fish with a "dolphin-safe" logo can help. This means the nets used to catch that tuna are designed to prevent cetaceans from becoming trapped in them. Similarly, if people stop buying commercial whale meat, the demand

Many volunteer groups spend a lot of time and money to help protect and rescue whales that are in trouble.

During a meeting of the International Whaling Commission, these Alaskans dressed up in whale costumes to call attention to the harm that commercial whaling does to whale populations.

for the meat will go down, and fewer whales will be killed for their meat.

Volunteering with a conservation group that helps whales is also another option. Many people write letters and help to educate people about whales through these conservation groups' programs. Talking to lawmakers about how to save the whales can also help.

Being mindful of the products you use and throw away is also important. Avoid balloon launches. When people release balloons into the air, they can easily end up in the oceans. If whales or other marine animals eat these balloons, they may become sick and even die. Cut

Perhaps one day all whale species will be completely safe in the oceans, free from the threat of endangerment.

up the plastic rings from six-packs of cans. Marine animals can get trapped in these and die, leaving less food for whales. Or, a whale could accidentally eat the six-pack ring whole, which can make it sick or kill it.

Organizing a clean-up outing may also help. Many types of pollution eventually end up in our oceans, which can make whales sick. Many conservation groups gather volunteers who help to pick up litter, especially along beaches, creeks, and rivers.

Though most people will never see or interact with these giant marine mammals, everybody can do something to help protect them. If laws are not passed and changes are not made to protect the environment, many whale populations could disappear forever.

GLOSSARY

baleen—A tough material that forms plates in the mouths of some types of whales.

blowhole—A nostril on the top of a whale's head through which it breathes air. Some whales have two blowholes on the top of their heads.

blubber—Fat layers found beneath the whale's skin. Blubber helps protect the whale from cold waters.

bycatch—Any animal caught in fishing nets not intended for it. For example, whales caught in tuna nets are bycatch.

calf—A baby whale.

cetacean—The scientific name for whales, dolphins, and porpoises.

conservation—The act of preserving or saving something, such as an animal or habitat. People who do this are called conservationists.

endangered—At risk of disappearing forever.

extinct—No longer existing.

krill—Small, shrimp-like marine animals that baleen whales use as food.

mammal—A warm-blooded animal that breathes air, gives birth to live young, has hair, and nurses its young with milk.

migrating—Traveling from one area to another, usually according to the seasons.

pod—A group of whales.

prey—Animals that are hunted and used as food.

species—A specific type of animal. For example, humpback whales are a species of whales.

threatened—At risk of becoming endangered.

FIND OUT MORE

Books

Hoyt, Erich. *Whale Rescue: Changing the Future for Endangered Wildlife*. Richmond Hill, Ontario: Firefly Books, 2005.

Nicklin, Flip and Linda Nicklin. *Face to Face with Whales*. Washington, DC: National Geographic, 2008.

Pringle, Laurence. *Whales! Strange and Wonderful.* Honesdale,
      PA: Boyds Mill Press, 2003.

Web Sites

Whales-NOAA Fisheries

http://www.nmfs.noaa.gov/pr/education/whales.htm

Learn more about eight different species of whales on the National
Oceanic & Atmospheric Administration Web site for kids.

Save the Whales

http://savethewhales.org

Save the Whales online offers information about endangered whales and
how to help.

Whale Watch

http://www.whalewatch.com/kids

The Whale Watch Web site has a lot of fun activities to learn more about
whales, including puzzles, quizzes, and fun facts.

INDEX

Page numbers in **boldface** are illustrations.

ABOUT THE AUTHOR

Johannah Haney is a freelance writer who lives with her husband Andrés in Boston. Just like the north Atlantic right whale, she travels to Florida every winter where she has swum in the ocean just a few feet away from dolphin pods. Johannah Haney has written several books for students, as well as many magazine articles.